ANIMAL GROUPS

HOW ANIMALS LIVE TOGETHER

WRITTEN BY ETTA KANER

ILLUSTRATED BY PAT STEPHENS

Kids Can Press

My thanks to my wonderful editor Stacey Roderick for her attention to detail and good sense of humor, to Pat Stephens for her amazing illustrations and to Marie Bartholomew for her creative design. Thank you also to Professor David L. Gibo from the Department of Zoology at the University of Toronto for his time and useful suggestions.

For Louise Singer, a true friend — EK
To Caitlin — PS

Text © 2004 Etta Kaner
Illustrations © 2004 Pat Stephens

All rights reserved. No part of this publication may be reproduced, stored in a retrieval system or transmitted, in any form or by any means, without the prior written permission of Kids Can Press Ltd. or, in case of photocopying or other reprographic copying, a license from The Canadian Copyright Licensing Agency (Access Copyright). For an Access Copyright license, visit www.accesscopyright.ca or call toll free to 1-800-893-5777.

Kids Can Press acknowledges the financial support of the Government of Ontario, through the Ontario Media Development Corporation's Ontario Book Initiative; the Ontario Arts Council; the Canada Council for the Arts; and the Government of Canada, through the BPIDP, for our publishing activity.

Published in Canada by
Kids Can Press Ltd.
29 Birch Avenue
Toronto, ON M4V 1E2

Published in the U.S. by
Kids Can Press Ltd.
2250 Military Road
Tonawanda, NY 14150

www.kidscanpress.com

Edited by Stacey Roderick
Designed by Marie Bartholomew

Printed in Hong Kong, China, by Book Art Inc., Toronto

The hardcover edition of this book is smyth sewn casebound. The paperback edition of this book is limp sewn with a drawn-on cover.

CM 04 0 9 8 7 6 5 4 3 2 1
CM PA 04 0 9 8 7 6 5 4 3 2 1

The map on page 37 appears courtesy of WorldAtlas.com.

National Library of Canada Cataloguing in Publication Data
Kaner, Etta
    Animal groups : how animals live together / written by Etta Kaner ; illustrated by Pat Stephens.
Includes index.
ISBN 1-55337-337-5 (bound).   ISBN 1-55337-338-3 (pbk.)

1. Social behavior in animals — Juvenile literature.
2. Animal behavior — Juvenile literature. I. Stephens, Pat
II. Title.

QL775.K35 2004   j591.56   C2002-905622-5

Kids Can Press is a ʟᴏʀᴜs™ Entertainment company

Contents

Introduction

Do you live in a group? Of course you do! It's called a family. Many animals live in a group, too. For example, some animals live in a family with their mother, father, brothers and sisters. Others may live in a harem, with a head male and many females. Or animals might live in a matriarchy, with a female leader of the group.

Why do animals live in groups? Living in groups helps animals survive. A group can help animals find food. They might hunt together, like hyenas, or share food, like coyotes. A group can help its members when they are sick or hurt. That's what a herd of elephants does. It's also easier to raise babies and keep safe in a group, as many birds do. And what about keeping clean? Group living is useful for that, too!

In this book you will find out how and why animals live together. You will learn about the different jobs animals do within their groups, such as being a babysitter, like a flamingo, or growing food, like leafcutter ants. And have you ever wondered why geese fly in a V or why monkeys always seem to be cleaning each other? You'll find out the answers to these and many other questions. So, just turn the page and join the group of animal fans.

Let's eat

Have you ever picked apples with your class or berries with your family? You probably got a lot more fruit as a group than if you had picked it by yourself. Some animals use the same strategy when it's time to eat. Lions and other meat-eating animals hunt for large prey in teams. Other animals help the group by sharing the food they catch. These leafcutter ants work together to grow food for their colony.

If you were a leafcutter ant ...

- you would eat a white fungus grown by your colony.
- you would do one of four jobs to help the fungus grow.
- you might carry freshly cut leaf pieces back to your nest.
- you might lick the leaves clean and then cut them up.
- you might chew the pieces into a mush.
- you might plant the mush in the garden, where it turns into fungus.

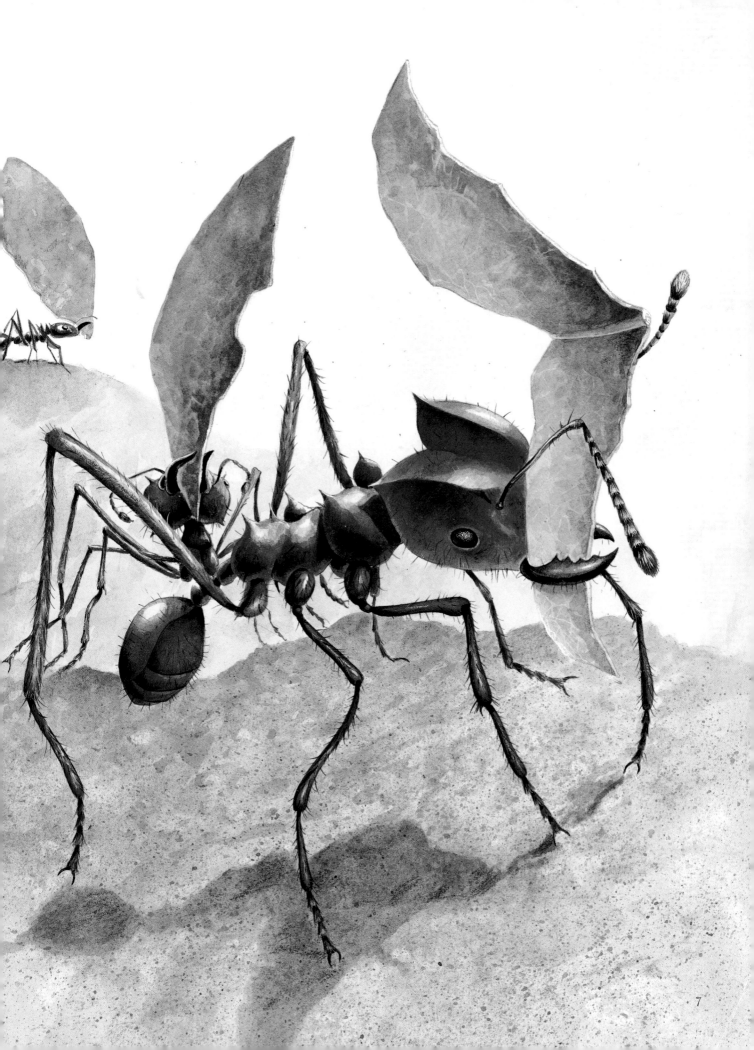

Hunting together

When a group of animals tries to catch food, its members have to cooperate. White pelicans work together as a flock to catch fish in shallow water. The pelicans form a line facing the shore. Paddling forward, they use their wings and feet to push more and more fish toward the shore. Finally, the pelicans form a circle, trapping the fish. Now it's easy for the pelicans to pick up fish with their huge beaks. And if a fish escapes from one beak, it will probably be scooped up by another one.

White pelicans

Striped marlin also hunt for fish in teams. When three or four of these ferocious fish find a group of smaller fish, they do something called "meatballing." The marlins harass the group from all sides, driving them into a tight bunch, or ball. Now the marlins can gobble up as many fish as they want. This is a lot easier than if each marlin were to chase individual fish.

Striped marlins

When smaller animals hunt for much larger prey, teamwork is a must. This is especially true for African hunting dogs, which eat antelopes. Hunting in a group called a pack, the dogs take turns chasing an antelope until the antelope becomes very tired. Then one dog grabs the antelope with its teeth and pulls it down. Once the antelope is on the ground, the rest of the pack is able to finish the job.

African hunting dogs

Helping each other out

Animals don't always need to hunt together to help each other find food. Ants lay down scent trails to lead other ants to food. Honeybees tell other bees about food sources by doing a special dance. And many birds collect food for group members.

The Florida scrub jay lives in scrubland, where there are very few trees and food is scarce. It takes many adult jays to find enough food to feed a nest full of babies. So, when jays grow up, they stay with their family. They help find

food and defend their younger siblings, or brothers and sisters, against snakes. Other birds, such as wrens, moorhens and woodpeckers, help their families the same way.

Florida scrub jays

Great leaping birds!

When a flock of cattle egrets forages for food, it looks like it's playing a game of leapfrog. The flock divides into two groups. The back group jumps over the front group to catch insects. This stirs up many more insects from the tall grasses. These insects fly up and are caught by the group following close behind. In this way, the cattle egrets all get their fair share of food.

Egrets

Coyote parents also have older "helpers" who bring food to the pups, or babies, in the family. This usually happens when the father is away hunting for food. Once the young are grown, however, coyotes might not stay together as a family. It all depends on the kind of food that is available.

If the food is large carrion, an animal that is already dead, coyotes stick together in their pack. Since the pack only shares with its members, they might have to defend their food from another pack before settling down to a meal. How do they do this? They make themselves look fierce. They bush out their thick fur and tails to look bigger, and they show their sharp pointed teeth.

Coyotes

11

All for one and one for all

What does an animal do when it's sick or hurt or in danger? It often depends on other animals in its group for help. The sick animal might live in a colony with thousands of members, like some birds. Or it might be part of an extended family, like these dwarf mongooses. But no matter what kind of group they live in, animals find help from their group members.

If you were a dwarf mongoose ...

- you would live in an extended family with your parents and about nine siblings.
- you would live in a vacant termite hill.
- if you were a male, you would take turns watching out for hawks while your family forages, or looks, for food.
- if you were a female, you would nurse and take care of the babies in your family, even if you're not their mother.

Strength in numbers

Many animals protect themselves by living in groups. As a group, even small animals can attack a larger predator. This is called mobbing. Different animals mob in different ways.

Ground squirrels use mobbing to get rid of snakes. A group of squirrels rushes at a threatening snake and throws sand in its face. Sometimes the really brave ones quickly bite the snake's body.

Ground squirrels

Gulls

Gull families live in colonies with hundreds of other gulls. If a fox tries to grab a baby, many gulls swoop down, pecking at the fox's head until it runs away. Caciques also build their nests close together. If a monkey or a toucan tries to steal an egg or a chick, the birds quickly join together to drive it away.

Cacique nests

Baboon

A troop of baboons will gang up on an attacking leopard. The baboons show their teeth and screech loudly. They bang and stamp their feet on the ground. Even a fierce leopard is frightened off by such a performance. Wouldn't you be?

Owl attack

Small birds will mob an owl even if they are not under attack. If they see an owl sitting quietly in a tree during the day, the birds fly close to the owl and call loudly. Soon all kinds of birds join in. Some buzz around the owl's head. Others might jab at its eyes. Still others dive-bomb it. Finally, the owl leaves. Why all the fuss? Small birds have a great fear of owls, who are one of their worst enemies. They hope that the owl will not want to return to their area.

Wilson's warbler

Female ruby-throated hummingbird

Long-eared owl

Gray jay

Male ruby-throated hummingbird

Northern Parula warbler

Song sparrow

Lending a helping hand

When animals are hurt or in danger, they need help just like you do. But that help doesn't come from a doctor or the police. It comes from the members of the group in which they live. Sometimes this even means risking their lives to help others.

Elephants live in a herd that is a matriarchy, a group led by a female. The herd supports its members in many ways. If a young calf falls while on the move, the whole herd stops. It helps the mother with her calf before moving again. If the herd is attacked, it bunches together. The matriarch, or head elephant, stands in front with the calves and older elephants safely behind her. If an elephant is shot, the herd runs to help the wounded elephant rather than away from the hunter.

Zebras live in a herd called a harem. A harem is a group of females and young led by a single male. The stallion, or male leader, looks out for the group's safety. When zebras travel, the stallion stays at the rear of the group. If any are separated, the stallion searches for them. If a sick or old zebra can't keep up with a traveling group, the whole group slows down.

Zebras

Name that group

You have probably heard of a "litter of puppies" or a "herd of cattle." But you might be surprised by some of the names scientists give to groups of wild animals. Try to match the group names with the animals listed on this page. Hint: Most of them can be found in this book.

Group name	Animal

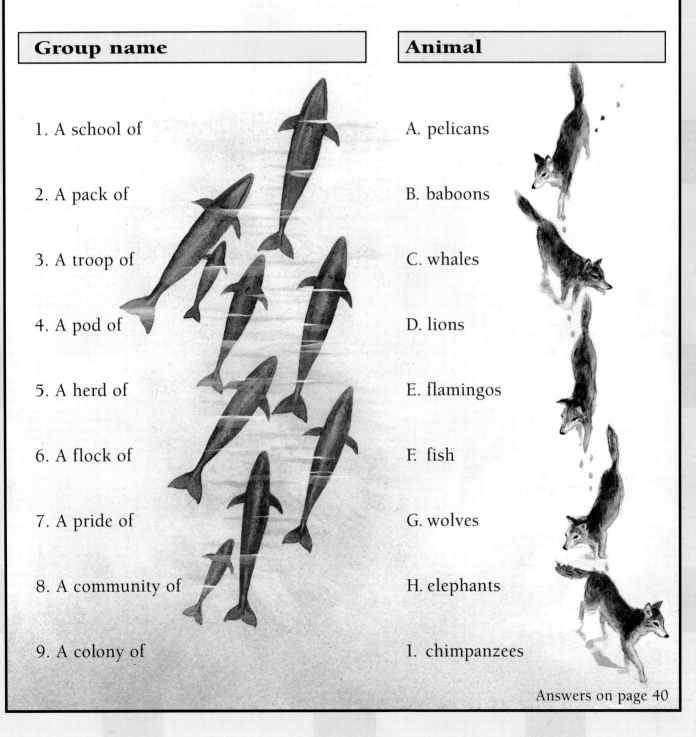

1. A school of

2. A pack of

3. A troop of

4. A pod of

5. A herd of

6. A flock of

7. A pride of

8. A community of

9. A colony of

A. pelicans

B. baboons

C. whales

D. lions

E. flamingos

F. fish

G. wolves

H. elephants

I. chimpanzees

Answers on page 40

Bringing up baby

Raising children is not an easy job for animal parents. They have to find enough food for their young and protect them from predators. They also need to teach their young how to become independent. Many animals work together to share this heavy load. Some animals raise their babies in two-parent families. Others do it in extended families. And some animals, like these flamingos, care for their offspring in crèches, or nurseries.

If you were a flamingo ...

- your family would live in a colony of thousands.
- you would teach your baby to recognize your voice by pressing your head against the hatching egg and calling to your chick.
- you would feed your chick a nutritious red liquid that comes from glands in your throat.
- your chick, along with hundreds of other chicks, would be cared for in a crèche by babysitter flamingos when you are away hunting for food.

19

Family matters

Many animals live in families. The family members often help look after the young.

Cichlids have as many as two hundred babies in their families at one time! Even before the young are born, both mother and father take turns caring for their eggs. They fan the eggs with their fins and tails to give them oxygen. They also move their eggs from place to place to protect them against predators. And once the fry, or young, are born, both parents make sure they don't swim too far away on their own.

South American marmosets have only two babies at a time. But each newborn is 1/4 of its mother's weight. It's almost impossible for her to carry around such heavy babies while she forages for food. So the father and older siblings help by carrying them instead—piggyback.

Gibbon parents also share the child rearing. A mother gibbon carries her child around her waist until it is two years old. Then the father takes over its care and training. At about this time, the mother usually gives birth again. Now she is able to give all of her attention to her new baby.

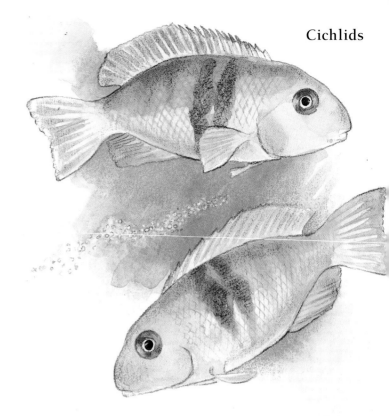

Cichlids

South American marmosets

Gibbons

A drink in the desert

The sandgrouse lives in the desert, far away from water. This isn't a problem for the adult sandgrouse. It can fly as far as 32 km (20 mi.) to find water. But what about the chicks? They can't fly. So their father brings them water in a very unusual way. While he drinks, he soaks his fluffed-up breast feathers in the water. When he returns to the nest, the chicks take turns sucking the water from his feathers.

Animal day care

Imagine what it would be like to have five hundred playmates at your babysitter's. That is what it's like for eider ducks. Eider duck babies join a crèche soon after they are born. They are protected there by a few adult females, called aunties, while their mothers go off to feed. If a threatening gull appears, the aunties sound an alarm and the chicks quickly gather around them. If the gull comes too close, an auntie grabs it by the leg and pulls it under the water.

Young elands also live in large nurseries with as many as four hundred other calves. The calves stay in this group until they're two years old. They spend a lot of time licking each other's fur. Elands do this only when they are young to feel close to each other.

Eider ducks

Elands

The babies of Patagonian cavies live in much smaller nurseries. You probably wouldn't see more than 20 young in one nursery. In fact, you might not see them at all. This is because the nursery is in a burrow in the ground. The strange thing is that the adults never enter the burrow. When a mother cavy wants to feed her babies, she whistles at the opening. A dozen young cavies might come out, but only two of them are hers. She leads her own babies away from the crowd to feed them in peace and quiet.

Bottlenose dolphins have babysitters the moment they are born. Actually, these are female dolphins that act like midwives. Midwives help mothers give birth. Dolphin midwives help the mother bring the calf, or baby, up to the water's surface so that it can breathe. They also protect the mother and her newborn calf from predators. When the calf is older, the mother leaves it with two or three watchful babysitters while she swims off to feed. Her calf plays with other calves while the babysitters circle around to protect them from enemies.

Patagonian cavies

Let's play

What games do you like to play with your friends? Tag? Follow the leader? King of the hill? Believe it or not, some animals play these and other games, too. Usually, young animals play with each other. But sometimes mothers and fathers join in. Playing together teaches young animals how to cooperate and builds friendships with others in their group. It also helps animals, such as these wolf pups, practice skills that they will need as adults.

If you were a young gray wolf ...

- you would live in a group called a pack.
- your pack would have two leaders — a male and a female.
- you would play with your five or six brothers and sisters.
- you would chase, ambush and play fight with each other. While play fighting, you would wag your tail to show that you're just playing.

Games animals play

King of the hill

Some animals play king of the hill. They scramble up a hill and try to pull down whoever is on top. Penguin chicks use a pile of ice or even a sleeping seal as their hill. Their climbing and pushing is practice for escaping from enemies. Young California sea lions use a boulder or rocky ledge as their hill. Their shoving prepares them for defending territories when they become adults.

California sea lions

Play fighting

When animals play fight, they might bite, claw, slap or push. But they don't use their full strength because they don't want to hurt each other. They are just practicing skills that they will need to use when they meet an enemy or a rival. Male polar bears stand on their hind legs and push and swat with their paws. They often do this with a play-fighting partner. These play-fighting partners also travel together during the summer and fall.

Polar bears

Tag

Tag is a favorite of most animals that play. They take turns chasing and being chased. When young gazelles play tag, they get to practice their high-speed running. This is important when escaping from predators. Young gibbons chase each other through the treetops in a follow-the-leader game. They do this for fun, but the game also helps strengthen their muscles.

Gazelles

Just hanging around

When young baboons play, they like to fall out of trees. They climb up a tree and hang by one hand at the end of a branch. Then they let themselves fall. When several baboons play this game, they try to push each other off the branch.

Play signals

Imagine that you are a puppy. You want to play with another puppy. What do you do? You crouch down with your head near the ground and your rear up in the air. This position is your play signal. It tells your friend that you want to play. It also tells your friend that any fighting is just pretend.

Without play signals, an animal might think that it was being attacked and would immediately defend itself. This would lead to fighting within the group, which is something that animals want to avoid.

Different animals have different play signals. Polar bears wag their heads quickly from side to side. Coyotes roll and squirm. Mongooses whip their tails. Badgers do little head thrusts. Tigers, lions and other cats swat and push each other.

Dog

Mongoose

Badger

Tigers

Playing together

When animals play games, they learn to work together. This is important when living in a group. People can also learn to cooperate through play. Why not try these games with a friend and find out how?

Up and down

1. Sit on the floor, facing each other.

2. Bend your knees, feet flat on the floor with toes touching.

3. Lean forward and grab each other's hands.

4. Stand up at the same time by pulling on each other. Now try to sit back down.

Back to back

1. Sit on the floor, back to back with your knees bent.

2. By pushing against each other's back and without moving your feet, stand up together.

3. Now sit back down together.

4. Try standing up halfway and walking sideways like a crab. Can you walk forward or backward in the same way?

Cleanup time

Animals keep themselves very clean. True or false? If you answered "true," you were right! Animals groom, or clean, themselves or each other every day. They pick out dirt, dead skin and parasites, such as fleas, lice and ticks from their fur or feathers. This helps keep them healthy.

When animals groom each other, scientists call it allogrooming. Allogrooming allows animals to clean those hard-to-reach places. It is also important for building friendships in a group. Some animals, such as these chimpanzees, spend several hours a day grooming each other.

If you were a chimpanzee ...

- you would live in a large group called a community.
- you would pick out parasites from your grooming partner's fur and eat them.
- you would use a pointed twig like a toothpick to clean your partner's teeth.
- you would remove splinters from your partner's skin with your fingers or lips.

Great groomers

If you watch a troop of gorillas groom each other, here's what you'll see. Mothers groom their young. The young groom the silverback, who is the male leader of the group. The silverback doesn't groom anyone. This order tells you that animals don't groom each other just to keep clean. Grooming also strengthens friendships and reminds animals of their position in the group. When young gorillas groom the silverback, they are saying, "Please be friendly to me." By not grooming anyone, the silverback is saying, "I'm the boss."

Gorillas

Female lions

Lions also groom each other in a certain order. Lions live in a pride of several males, females and young. Females use their rough bumpy tongues to groom the males, other females and their cubs. But the male lions don't groom anyone but themselves.

Coatis

Coatis use their teeth to groom each other. They sit in a line head to tail, and gently nibble all over each other's bodies.

Birds of a feather groom together

Picture this. Two birds are standing next to each other. One bird tilts its head back and ruffles up its neck feathers. Does it have a sore neck? No! It's just asking its partner to clean its hard-to-reach spots. As soon as the partner sees this position, it gets to work.

Coming together

Sometimes animals gather in very large groups called aggregations. An aggregation can have as many as a thousand or even a million members in it. Why would animals want to be part of such a large crowd? They might be looking for food or a mate. They may be gathering together for safety or to hibernate. Or they might be migrating, or moving, from one place to another, like these monarch butterflies.

If you were a monarch butterfly ...

- you would live alone during the summer.
- in late summer and autumn, you would start to migrate south to Mexico.
- as you migrate, there would be more and more monarchs moving in the same direction. Soon, you would be migrating with millions of others.
- during the winter, you would live in evergreen trees covered with monarchs. By being part of such a large group, you would have a better chance of surviving an attack by a predator.

On the move

Most animals that migrate move in an aggregation. Migrating in a crowd has definite advantages. When ducks and geese fly south for the winter, the group flies in a V. The wing tips of each bird move the air in circles. By following close behind and off to one side of each other, all the birds except the leader can use the air circles for extra lift. This means that each bird needs less energy for flying.

Geese

Swallows and swifts use rising warm air called thermals to give them extra lift. Hawks and falcons use these same thermals to help them migrate and to prey on the smaller birds. Fortunately, when small birds fly in a large group, there is less of a chance of an individual bird becoming a predator's dinner.

Migrating in an aggregation makes it safer for spiny lobsters, too. Spiny lobsters walk in long lines along the sea bottom when they migrate. They walk into deeper water so that they will be safe from winter storms. If they meet a predator, they quickly make a circle with their claws facing outward.

Who would want to tackle a group like that?

Spiny lobsters

Flyways and byways

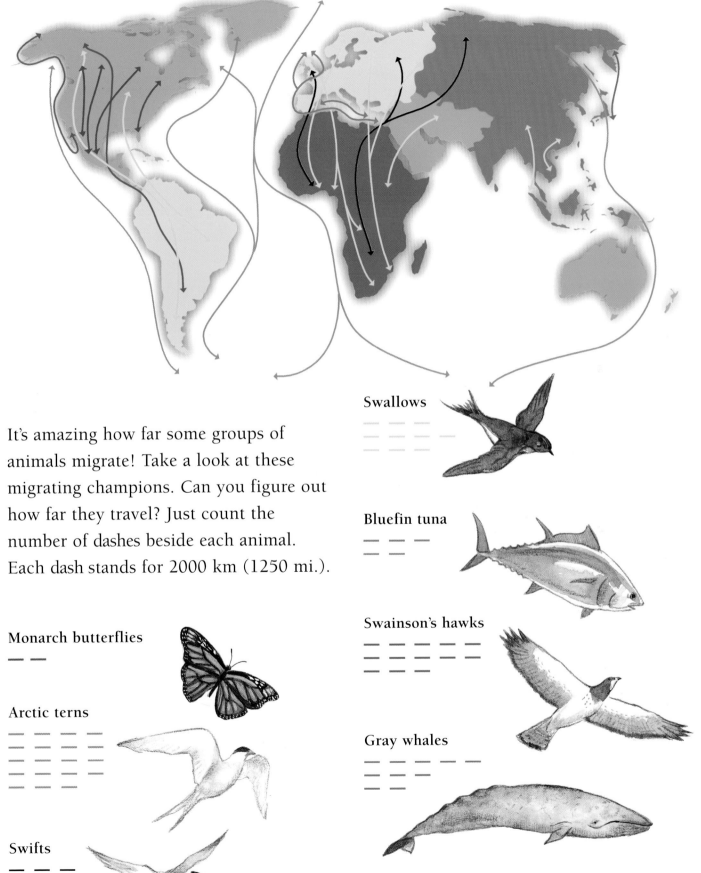

It's amazing how far some groups of animals migrate! Take a look at these migrating champions. Can you figure out how far they travel? Just count the number of dashes beside each animal. Each dash stands for 2000 km (1250 mi.).

Swallows
‒ ‒ ‒ ‒

Bluefin tuna
‒ ‒ ‒

Swainson's hawks
‒ ‒ ‒ ‒ ‒
‒ ‒ ‒ ‒ ‒
‒ ‒

Gray whales
‒ ‒ ‒ ‒
‒ ‒

Monarch butterflies
‒ ‒

Arctic terns
‒ ‒ ‒ ‒
‒ ‒ ‒ ‒
‒ ‒ ‒ ‒

Swifts
‒ ‒ ‒
‒

Answers on page 40

37

Follow the crowd

If you've ever thrown seeds for birds, you probably noticed that only a few birds came to eat at first. But before you knew it, you probably had more birds than you wanted. You had an aggregation of birds! This happens in the wild, too, and not just with birds.

Ladybugs

When fish or mammals find food, it's not long before dozens of others join them. How do they learn about the food? They may have been on the lookout for something tasty to eat or they may have seen other animals moving toward the food.

Winter weather is another reason why some animals become part of an aggregation. Both ladybugs and snakes hibernate during the winter. Ladybugs gather together by the hundreds or thousands under a rock or log on a south-facing slope to keep warm and moist. Snakes do the same. Some even roll up with as many as several hundred snakes in a huge ball.

Snakes

Penguins don't hibernate during the winter, but they certainly huddle together in large numbers to keep warm. During a blizzard, as many as five thousand Emperor penguins will pack tightly together for warmth. The inside of the huddle is much warmer than the outside. When penguins near the outer edge of the huddle become too cool, they try to move toward the center. As the warmer penguins get pushed toward the outside, they begin to cool down. Then they start moving toward the middle, and so on.

All in a bunch

If you ever see a large swarm of mosquitoes hovering in the air, you can be sure that it's a bunch of males waiting for some females to come along. It's easier for female mosquitoes to find a mate when a male is part of a large group.

Index

Answers

Page 17:
1-F, 2-G, 3-B, 4-C, 5-H, 6-A, 7-D, 8-I, 9-E

Page 37:
Monarch butterflies, 4000 km (2500 mi.)
Arctic terns, 38 000 km (23 750 mi.)
Swifts, 16 000 km (10 000 mi.)
Swallows, 20 000 km (12 500 mi.)
Bluefin tuna, 10 000 km (6250 mi.)
Swainson's hawks, 26 000 km (16 250 mi.)
Gray whales, 20 000 km (12 500 mi.)